ONE
RAINY
DAY

PATRICIA LEE GAUCH, EDITOR

Copyright © 2002 by Valeri Gorbachev. All rights reserved. This book, or parts thereof,
may not be reproduced in any form without permission in writing from the publisher,
PHILOMEL BOOKS,
a division of Penguin Putnam Books for Young Readers,
345 Hudson Street, New York, NY 10014. Philomel Books,
Reg. U.S. Pat. & Tm. Off. Published simultaneously in Canada.
Printed in Hong Kong by South China Printing Co. (1988) Ltd.
Book design by Semadar Megged.
The text is set in 17-point Worcester Round.
The art for this book was completed with pen-and-ink and watercolors.
Library of Congress Cataloging-in-Publication Data
Gorbachev, Valeri.   One rainy day / written and illustrated by Valeri Gorbachev.   p. cm.
Summary: A pig and various other animals crowd under a tree to escape the rain.
[1. Pigs–Fiction. 2. Rain and rainfall–Fiction. 3. Animals–Fiction. 4. Counting.
5. Humorous stories.] I. Title.   PZ7.G6475 On 2002   [E]–dc21   2001036659
ISBN 0-399-23628-7
1 3 5 7 9 10 8 6 4 2
First Impression

To my wife,
Victoria,
for her patience and support.

ONE RAINY DAY

written and illustrated by

Valeri Gorbachev

PHILOMEL BOOKS • NEW YORK

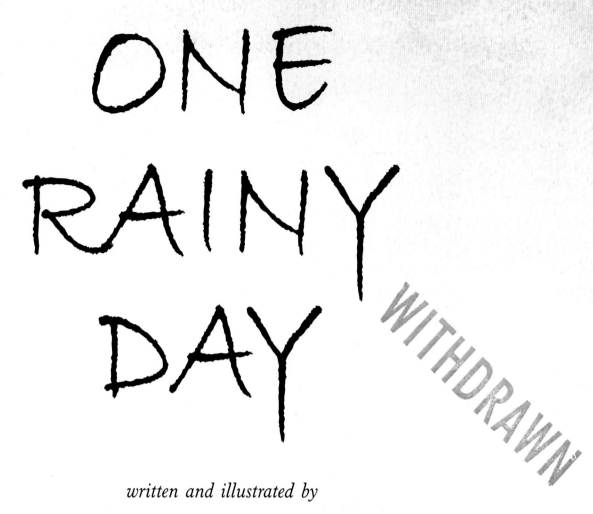

What happened to you, friend Pig? I can see you're wet. Let me guess. You went to the meadow to get some flowers and you were caught in the rain. Is that right?"

"Yes."

"You must have forgotten to take an umbrella. But why didn't you hide under a tree?"

"I did."

"But then, why did you get wet,
friend Pig?"

"Because, to escape the rain, a small—
very fast—mouse ran right under the tree,
too."

"Surely there was enough room for you and the small—very fast—mouse."

"Yes, but then two porcupines joined us."

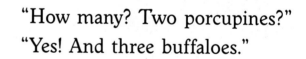

"How many? Two porcupines?"
"Yes! And three buffaloes."

"Did I hear you right? Three buffaloes?"
"Yes! And four leopards came after them."

"What did you say? Four leopards?"
"You heard me! And five lions came next,
under the same tree."
"I can't imagine! Five lions?"

"Yes! And after that, six gorillas ran
under the tree to escape from the rain."
"Are you sure? Six gorillas?"

"Yes! And seven crocodiles followed them."

"Oh, no! Seven crocodiles?"

"Yes, and then eight hippopotamuses
came to that same tree."
"I can't believe it! Eight hippopotamuses?"

"Yes, and then nine rhinoceroses came running."
"That is terrible, nine rhinoceroses."

"I know. Then ten elephants also ran under the tree."

"Wow! Ten elephants?

"Ah, friend Pig, I get it. With all
ten elephants,
nine rhinoceroses,
eight hippopotamuses,
seven crocodiles,
six gorillas,
five lions,
four leopards,
three buffaloes,
two porcupines,
and one fast mouse
all under the tree,
there was no room for you. Am I right?"

"No! There was room for everyone."
"Then I don't get it. Why were you so wet?"

"Because when the rain was over . . .

" . . . I was in such a hurry to get home to tell you about what happened to me on this rainy day that I didn't miss a single puddle!"